Can We Have Our Ball Back?

Created by Keith Chapman

First published in Great Britain by HarperCollins Children's Books in 2007

1 3 5 7 9 10 8 6 4 2

ISBN-13: 978-0-00-722596-5
ISBN-10: 0-00-722596-2

Based on the television series *Fifi and the Flowertots* and the
original script 'Can We Have Our Ball Back?' by Dave Ingham
© Chapman Entertainment Limited 2007

Printed and bound in China

Can We Have Our Ball Back?

HarperCollins *Children's Books*

Fifi Forget-Me-Not
was happily hanging out
her washing when a big juicy
blackcurrant came **SPLAT!**
flying through the air
and hit the nice
clean sheets.

"Buttercups and
Daisies!" cried Fifi
as she looked down
into the garden.

Stingo and Slugsy
stared back up at her.
"Can we have our ball back
please?" they shouted up to Fifi.

"I should have known," she said, looking at her ruined
washing. "You can have your ball back when you
clean up this mess!"

The naughty pair looked at each other. "Time to go, my
slimy friend!" said Stingo, buzzing off out the garden.

"Ohh... Fiddly Flowerpetals!" sighed Fifi.

Over at Honeysuckle
House, Bumble and Pip
were playing football too.
"Isn't football great?"
Pip said, passing to Bumble.

"Well, I've never actually
played before," Bumble said,
nervously tapping
the ball back.

Pip dribbled the ball all the way down
the garden and passed to Bumble
who stuck his foot out to score and...
sneezed a **giant** sneeze, making
the ball fly up, up and out
of the garden.

Not far away,
Slugsy and Stingo were
moping around. "I wish we had
our ball back," Slugsy sniffed, miserably.

"Yeah," nodded Stingo, "but I'm
not washing Fifi's sheets!"

Just then, Bumble's football
came flying in and bopped
Slugsy on the head!

"You'll have to get it off me first!" said Stingo, dribbling the ball around Pip. "I'm the best footballer in the whole garden!"

"No you're not!" said Pip, who really just wanted his ball back. "Bumble is, he's got a **rocket shot!**" Stingo and Slugsy looked at each other and burst out laughing. **"BUMBLE?"**

"He can beat anyone,"
Pip said proudly.

"Alright then," said Stingo, still chuckling.
"Let's have a match this afternoon."

Pip was just agreeing to the match
as Bumble buzzed into the garden.
"What are they laughing at?"
he asked Pip.

"We're going to play football against Stingo
and Slugsy this afternoon," Pip announced to a
shocked Bumble. "We'll win easily with your rocket shot!"
And with that, Pip dashed off to get some last minute practise.

"But Pip!" Bumble called. "I don't know how to play!"
He kicked the ground sadly as Fifi trundled up in Mo.

Soon the two tots were kicking the ball all over the garden. On the deck of his Apple House, Stingo watched Fifi and Bumble through his spyglass and laughed. "They're terrible," he said to Slugsy. "And if they can't win, why don't we play for a prize?

A big, fat, sticky prize..."

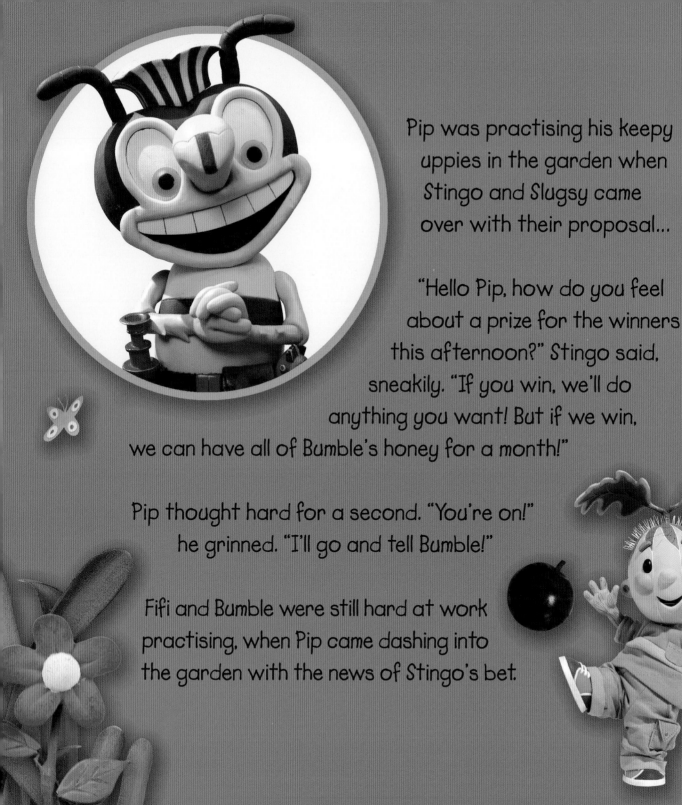

Pip was practising his keepy uppies in the garden when Stingo and Slugsy came over with their proposal...

"Hello Pip, how do you feel about a prize for the winners this afternoon?" Stingo said, sneakily. "If you win, we'll do anything you want! But if we win, we can have all of Bumble's honey for a month!"

Pip thought hard for a second. "You're on!" he grinned. "I'll go and tell Bumble!"

Fifi and Bumble were still hard at work practising, when Pip came dashing into the garden with the news of Stingo's bet.

"Oh no!" wailed Bumble. "A whole month's honey!

"But we are going to win, aren't we, Bumble?" asked Pip, hopefully.

"Of course you are," smiled Fifi, looking at a rather worried Bumble.

Soon it was time for the match. Two goals had been set up at either end of the clearing and Violet, Primrose and Fifi were all lined up, ready to cheer on Bumble and Pip.

Stingo and Slugsy ran on to the pitch, clapping themselves and stretching elaborately before Bumble and Pip jogged on to the Flowertot's applause.

Poppy, the referee, was waiting in the middle of the pitch. "May the best team win!" she declared, popping the ball down.

"That'll be us then!"

Stingo smirked at Slugsy.

As soon as the ball was back
in play, Pip was after Stingo.
He slide tackled the tricky
wasp but managed to run
right into Bumble as the
ball rolled into their goal.

Two minutes, later, Stingo
planted another goal right
over Bumble's head.

"Half time!"
Poppy blew her whistle hard.

"We haven't even scored!" complained Pip.
"We need your rocket shot, Bumble!"

Bumble sighed. "But I just got pollen up my
nose when I kicked the ball!"

"Hmmm, that gives me an
idea," said Fifi, dashing off.

The second half had already started when Fifi came running on to the pitch with a bunch of big, bright flowers. "Here Bumble," she whispered, "have a sniff of this!"

"But it will make me sneeze!" Bumble said.

Fifi smiled. "Exactly!" Bumble took a big sniff of the flowers. As the ball came to Bumble, he "ATTISSCHHOO!" sneezed so hard, his foot kicked out and hit the football super hard.

It was a perfect rocket shot and flew right into the back of Slugsy's goal.

"We won?" said Pip as Bumble buzzed him up in a big hug.
"We won!"

"Hey, Stingo," said Bumble, as he tried to
sneak off. "Aren't you forgetting something?
Like doing anything we
asked if we won?"

In no time at all,
Stingo and Slugsy were
hanging out Fifi's newly
washed sheets. "Call yourself
a goalkeeper?" sniped Stingo.
"You couldn't catch a cold!"

Suddenly, a ball came
flying up on to the
roof and hit the clean sheets.

"Can we have our ball back,
please!" called Fifi and Bumble
from down in the garden.

"Very funny!" shouted Stingo
as the Flowertots fell
about laughing.

Make Your Own
Yummy Honey Footie Buns

After the football match, we ate
lots of these *yummy honey buns!*

You will need:

* 2 cups plain flour * 1/4 cup caster sugar
* 2 tsp baking powder * 1 tsp baking soda
* 1/2 tsp salt * 2 eggs
* 1/2 cup runny honey
* 1/2 cup orange juice
* 1/3 cup butter, melted
* 1 tsp vanilla extract
* 12 bun cases
* Always ask a grown-up to help you
melt the butter and use the oven!

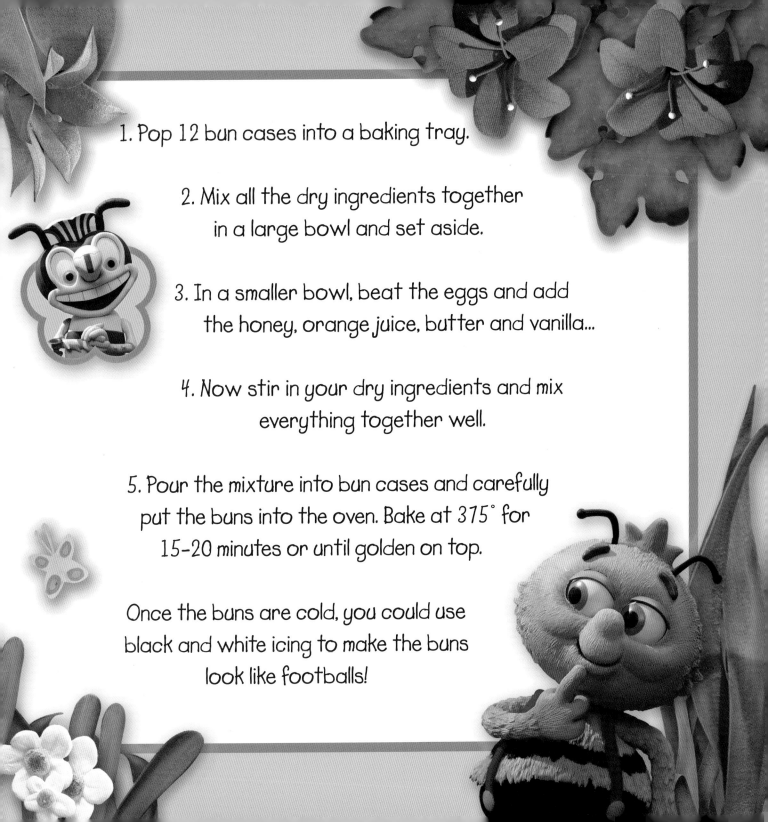

1. Pop 12 bun cases into a baking tray.

2. Mix all the dry ingredients together
in a large bowl and set aside.

3. In a smaller bowl, beat the eggs and add
the honey, orange juice, butter and vanilla...

4. Now stir in your dry ingredients and mix
everything together well.

5. Pour the mixture into bun cases and carefully
put the buns into the oven. Bake at 375° for
15-20 minutes or until golden on top.

Once the buns are cold, you could use
black and white icing to make the buns
look like footballs!